Printed in the United States of America
First Edition, 2014
Library of Congress Control Number: 2014914824

ISBN 978-0-692-27666-2

Charlie Buys
P.O. Box 752632
Las Vegas, NV 89136

TO MY FAMILY,

Thank you for always being there to believe in and love me, especially Ma & Ev. You guys mean more to me than you know. Thank you for teaching me to always dream bigger & never give up along the way. Love Always!

— T.C.B.

SCOTT THE SAN DIEGO SEA LION

To Ed, Jenny, Joseph 'Joey', Peter, Clare,
Catherine, & Marie,

Hope you enjoy reading it!

Love Always,

Charlie Buys

CHARLIE BUYS

In the waters of the San Diego Bay, there lived a sea lion named Scott. He had brown fur and a nose with a heart-shaped spot.

"My name is Scott," he said with a smile of glee. "Today I will find someone to play with me by the sea."

Then, Scott saw a funny sight. A pelican with a large beak was diving into the water from a great height. The bird came to the surface with a fish in her beak. Scott tried to say hello, but the fish was too big for the pelican to speak. The pelican flew beneath a blue bridge that crossed the bay. Scott swam after the pelican because he wanted to play.

The pelican landed by a seagull flock and Scott sat next to them on a great, big rock.

"Hello, my name is Scott. How do you do?"

"My name is Penelope. It's nice to meet you," she said as she looked down at the fish. "Mmm, this looks like a tasty dish!"

Just as Penelope was about to eat her lunch, the biggest seagull in the group ate her fish in one munch!

"You stole my food and that was rude."

"What are you going to do about it, big-nose?" the seagull said as he stood on his toes.

Feeling sad about what the seagull said, Penelope put her wings over her beak and flew away. She flew into the clouds above the bay. Scott swam over to the other bird. He was upset over what he had heard.

"My name is Scott, and you should say 'sorry' to Penelope. If you do, we can all become friends. I guarantee.

"My name is Sal and I will not be your pal. I am the fastest and strongest bird by the sea. I will not say sorry because you cannot make me."

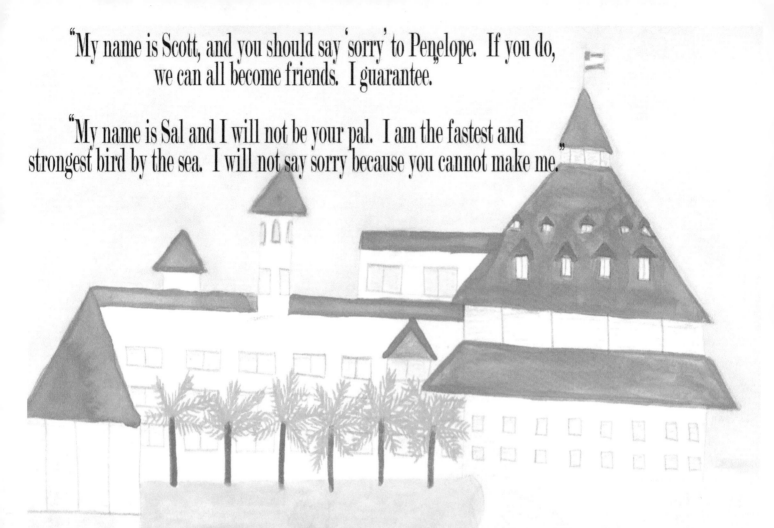

Scott knew what Sal did was not fair, but the seagull just did not care.

"We can have a race to see who is really fast. You will say sorry to Penelope if you come last."

"Okay," said Sal. "We will race to the flag on the back of that blue boat on the sea. You can bet the winner will be me."

Sal got ready for the race and Scott looked for Penelope all over the place. Scott saw her crying on a pier and swam to her to stop her from crying another tear.

"Are you okay?" asked Scott.

"No, I am not. I am not okay. Sal was mean to me today. He made fun of my beak and made me sad. If my beak were smaller, I would be glad."

"Your beak makes you different, and its great to be unique. In fact, I think it makes you look quite chic.

"I never thought being different was a good thing," Penelope said, as she stood up tall.

"I think it's alright to be me after all."

Scott and Penelope swam to Sal at the edge of the bay. Scott hoped he would have a lucky day. Penelope floated by the back of the boat and cleared her throat.

"On the count of three the race will begin. 1, 2, 3 ...Swim!"

Scott tried his best to swim fast. He did not want to be last. Scott could see Sal fly to the boat. Scott jumped out of the water and hoped he could float.

Scott grabbed the flag in a flash and landed in the water with a splash! Penelope was glad Scott won. Sal was sad because his greedy ways were done.

"I am sorry, Penelope. I was not the nicest bird in the sea. It was not nice to steal your food. It was not nice to be rude."

Sal shook Penelope's wing and flew away. All was quiet on the bay.

Scott gave her a hug and said happily, "You should never be afraid to stand up for yourself, Penelope. Every sea shell along the shore is different and so are we."

Scott and Penelope played some more, and that is how they became the best of friends by the shore.

S	H	E	L	L	F	P
M	E	T	S	S	P	E
B	E	A	C	H	S	L
O	L	O	L	S	O	I
A	T	F	A	I	T	C
T	M	P	M	F	O	A
C	H	O	C	E	A	N

find the words:

Beach, Boat, Clam, Fish, Ocean, Pelican, Sal, Scott, Shell, Sea Lion

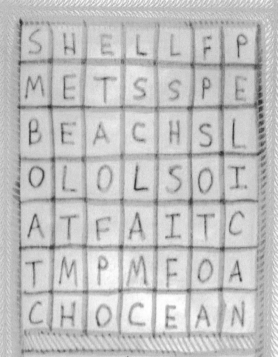

What is the difference Between Sea Lions and Seals?

- Seals do not have ears like sea lions. They listen with holes on each side of their head.

- Sea lions can use their back flippers to waddle on land, but seals can only crawl.

- Sea lions are louder and friendlier than seals.

- California sea lions like Scott have brown fur. Harbor seals have fur coats that can be gray, brown, black, or spotted.

CPSIA information can be obtained at www.ICGtesting.com
Printed in the USA
BVOW11s0530170914

367182BV00001B/1/P

9 780692 276662